A

ENCYCLOPEDIA BROWN'S
BOOK OF
WACKY CRIMES

Also by Donald J. Sobol

ENCYCLOPEDIA BROWN'S

BOOK OF

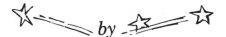WACKY CRIMES

by

Donald J. Sobol

illustrated by Ted Enik

LODESTAR BOOKS
E. P. Dutton   New York

The incidents in the news stories are true, but most of the names and places have been changed.

Library of Congress Cataloging in Publication Data

Sobol, Donald J., date
Encyclopedia Brown's book of wacky crimes.

"Lodestar books."
Summary: A detective shares his recorded collection of strange and funny criminal cases with his friends, changing names and places to protect the innocent.
1. Crime and criminals—United States—Anecdotes, facetiae, satire, etc.—Juvenile literature.
2. Detectives—United States—Anecdotes, facetiae, satire, etc.—Juvenile literature. [1. Crime and criminals—Wit and humor] I. Enik, Ted, ill.
II. Title. III. Title: Book of wacky crimes.
HV6789.S6 1982 364.1'0973 82-9683
ISBN 0-525-66786-5

Published in the United States by E. P. Dutton, Inc.,
2 Park Avenue, New York, N.Y. 10016
Published simultaneously in Canada by Clarke,
Irwin & Company Limited, Toronto and Vancouver
Editor: Virginia Buckley   Designer: Trish Parcell
Printed in the U.S.A.   First Edition
10 9 8 7 6 5 4 3 2 1

For
Lenore Appleson

Contents

ENCYCLOPEDIA BROWN'S
BOOK OF
WACKY CRIMES

A Rainy Day

Encyclopedia Brown liked being a detective. Even though he was only ten, he had never failed to solve a case.

When school let out for the summer, he had opened his own detective agency in the family garage. Business had been good, owing largely to Bugs Meany, Wilford Wiggins, and a few other teenagers who preyed upon the younger children of the neighborhood.

Tuesday morning Encyclopedia stood in the doorway of the Brown Detective Agency and watched a rainstorm pelt the roofs and streets of Idaville.

"Bugs Meany isn't likely to do any mischief in this weather," he commented.

"And Wilford Wiggins won't try any of his get-rich-quick schemes," said Sally Kimball, Encyclopedia's junior partner. "Wilford will just roll over and go back to sleep."

A silver branch of lightning flashed above the houses. Thunder cracked and faded, leaving the morning to the fierce wind and rain.

"We won't have any customers today unless they're dolphins," Encyclopedia said. Glumly he rested his hand on the garage-door handle.

"Wait, don't close up!" someone shouted.

Encyclopedia spied two of his pals, Charlie Stewart and Benny Breslin. They were halfway down the block and racing for shelter.

Slipping and sloshing, the two boys ducked into the Brown Detective Agency.

"Am I glad to get out of this fence-lifter," gasped Charlie, rubbing rainwater from his eyes with the sides of his fists.

"We were headed for a ball game in South Park when the sky went *schlurrp!*" panted Benny. "I've got water on the knee clear up to my scalp."

Encyclopedia fetched towels. He pitched them at his two friends.

"Thanks," Benny mumbled. "Another two blocks and I'd have drowned."

"Don't worry," Sally said. "The Coast Guard would have rescued you."

"Do you know," Benny replied, "that last year there were more members of the New York City Police Department than there were members of the United States Coast Guard?"

Instantly Charlie's face lit up. "Nearly fifty percent of all crimes are committed by people under eighteen," he announced.

"Ninety percent of all burglaries are the work of young people, thirteen to twenty-one years old," Sally said.

The game of facts was on.

Encyclopedia's friends had suspected for some time that he was secretly collecting oddities of crime from around the world. So they tried to remember everything on the subject that they read or heard. Once in a while, when they got together with nothing special to do, they played the game. They tossed out facts that they thought he could use. The fun lay in trying to come up with the strangest fact.

It was Benny's turn.

"How about this one?" he asked. "Nearly half of all bank robberies happen on Friday."

"Burglaries account for nearly three out of every ten crimes," Charlie shot back.

Benny didn't hesitate. "A stolen car is two hundred times more likely to get into a crash than other cars."

"Last year police across the nation issued about eighty-two thousand traffic tickets every day," Sally countered.

Charlie struggled to top that one. "Boston usually has the highest auto theft rate in the country," he said weakly.

"That's pretty feeble," Benny said, and further expressed his opinion by holding his nose.

Sally was looking confident. "The more sisters a boy

5

has," she said, "the less likely he is to become a juvenile delinquent."

Charlie and Benny were silenced. Sally had bested them, and they wavered on the edge of defeat. She followed up with the clincher.

"A woman who sees a theft being committed is more likely than a man to try to stop it," she declared.

"Where'd you learn that?" Charlie challenged.

"It was a University of Virginia study," Sally answered.

"You better not add that to your collection, Encyclopedia," Charlie warned. "It can't be true!"

"I won't use it," Encyclopedia promised.

"Why not?" demanded Sally, her voice rising in anger. "It's *true.*"

"Oh, I'm sure it is," Encyclopedia said. "But I'm not collecting facts."

Sally, Charlie, and Benny regarded him questioningly.

"You told me that you had already filled three notebooks," Sally protested.

"Yes, I have," Encyclopedia replied. "I've filled them with true cases and not bare facts—not just statistics. All the cases are . . . well, sort of wacky."

"Why didn't you stop us?" Benny answered.

"Because I enjoy listening to you," Encyclopedia answered. "Besides, the game keeps you reading."

"Maybe you would show us the kind of funny cases you're looking for," Sally suggested.

Encyclopedia took a large black book from a shelf. "This is my first notebook," he said. "It has the oldest cases."

He leafed through the pages. Many of the cases went back to the 1970s, and a few even farther. They were arranged by date and subject.

"Let's hear them," Charlie urged.

"I don't like crimes in which the crooks get away," Sally said. "It's wrong."

"Not every town is like Idaville," Charlie reminded her. "In some, the crooks do get away."

"But sooner or later almost all of them are caught," Encyclopedia said. He turned to the first page of his notebook.

Sally, Charlie, and Benny found comfortable places and settled down to listen.

Encyclopedia began to read. . . .

CHAPTER 1

Harebrained Heists

1947

Dear Diary. A Philadelphia husband-wife burglary team went to jail after police found the wife's diary. It contained such tidbits as: *February 23—John and I went out this evening, best ever—$24 cash, shoulder strap pocketbook, $5 pennies, an expensive dark gray fur coat for me.*

1969

Just one of those thins. Police in Vienna, Austria, couldn't figure out how locked homes were being burglarized—till they caught the culprit, a tiny (4-foot 9-inch) youth of 17. He entered through 9-by-12-inch mail slots.

1973

Red-haired Mrs. Nora McBride toughened her muscles as a steel cutter and dock worker in her native Wales. When she came to New York City, she wasn't about to let any hoodlum steal her hard-earned money.

A luckless mugger tried. McBride, 35, and the mother of two, decked him with two punches. Then she sat on his stomach with both hands around his throat.

While she was holding him down for the police, his partner snatched her purse.

Don't call me, I'll call you. A would-be robber drove into a Bay Village, Ohio, gas station, told the attendant he had a gun in his pocket, and demanded the cash.

The attendant, Frank Dwyer, refused. The pair argued until the robber threatened to call the police. Dwyer invited him to do just that and offered him free use of the telephone.

The robber called. The police came—and forthwith locked him up.

"I think we could chalk it up to his being a little bit stupid," police spokeswoman Sheila Chadwick said. "He probably just got utterly confused when things did not go the way he wanted."

No smarter was a youthful burglar who forced his way into a woman's apartment in Syracuse, New York. After roughing her up, he was suddenly gripped by remorse and inquired if he might be of some help.

"Call the police!" wailed the woman.

Call them he did—and was charged with burglary and assault.

After 74 pairs of shoes were stolen from a Connecticut shoe company, 37 pairs were found dumped a week later on the front lawn of the police chief. With the shoes was the note: *Sorry, no sizes fit.*

Disappointed by the lack of cash at a Detroit, Michigan, service station, a gunman wearing a ski mask pumped gas for ten minutes and made himself $45 before lighting out.

Susie Hahn, a 21-year-old house burglar, received three years in prison after police linked her to several break-ins in Little Rock, Arkansas.

Her fingerprints trapped her even though she'd been careful to wear gloves while practicing her calling.

The prosecution noted her poor choice of gloves. She had worn golf gloves, which have no fingertips.

1979

Harold Blake, 20, of Champaign, Illinois, was strolling through a local grocery store when a craving for dessert topping seized him. Opening a can, he squirted a dash of the topping into his mouth, put back the cap, replaced the can on the shelf, and left the store. The judge fined him $100.

Fancy pants. A 27-year-old upstate New York man fancied a pair of pants in an apartment he was burglarizing. He put them on and left behind his old pair—with his name in them.

Why had he written his name in his pants?

"There are too many thieves around," he confided to the police. "I didn't want anyone stealing them."

Fleeing from a store in Nashville, Tennessee, with $383 in loot, holdup man Joe Arsenis, 23, glanced back to see who was chasing him, ran smack into a concrete pole, and knocked himself cuckoo. Sentence: five years.

A young macho swaggered into a fast-food eatery in Saint Ann, Missouri, and told the countergirl he had a gun in his pocket. "The cash, sweetie," he commanded.

She replied, *"Aw gedouttahere!"*

Cowed, he ordered two hamburgers and a large French fries.

Next, please? Clerk Betty Herman was alone in the convenience store in New Orleans, Louisiana, when two men entered, wagged a knife, and ordered her into a storeroom.

While one man guarded her, the other man took over the counter and waited on customers. The store was busy, but he handled the work with ease. After an hour, the pair escaped with $100.

On the money. A gunman stepped into a liquor store in Laramie, Wyoming, knowing what he wanted: $125—no more, no less. He needed the sum, he said, to pay a fine or be sent to jail. And that's all he took.

Donald Majors of Richland, Washington, refused to turn over a nickel to the robber who came into his gas station.

Impressed, the robber put away his gun and shook hands. "You've got a lot of guts," he said. He wished Majors good luck and departed.

"I didn't know what I was doing when I told him no," Majors said weakly.

Dave Cutler, a laundromat operator in Venice, California, forked over his wallet to a masked gunman.

"I was touched," Cutler said of the robber, who fished out only four dollars and tossed back the wallet. "He seemed to want so little. So before he could walk away, I asked if I could say a little prayer for him—and, you know, he dropped the four dollars and ran away screaming."

An 18-year-old Ontario man held up a 7-Eleven store, but fell prey to his stomach. After relieving a clerk and three customers of their money, he ordered the clerk to make and wrap 30 sandwiches. The police arrived ahead of the takeout order.

CLINKLE

1980

Sorry about that. A man accused of holding up a store in Houston, Texas, at least eight times in three weeks—and on two occasions, twice in the same day—asked the police for a break.

"I never took more than twenty-five or fifty dollars," he protested. "And besides, you can ask the man. I always apologized when I robbed him."

You can't throw the book at 'em. Three times in two years thieves filched the book containing all the state's criminal laws from the library in Waterford, Connecticut.

Tell me not in mournful numbers. In a Decatur, Georgia, tavern, a man pulled a gun and passed his hat around. When he got it back, he dumped the collection of coins and bills on the floor and grumbled, "If that's all you have in here, you people should be robbing me."

Leaving the money, he pocketed his gun, put on his hat, and stomped out.

Three masked gunmen, innocent of the ways of toddlers, flubbed a robbery attempt at a South Carolina day-care center. At the sight of the masks, the preschoolers started bawling up a storm. The gunmen became flustered and took off.

Be it ever so humble. The Dowling Brass Company of Trenton, New Jersey, paid $100,000 for a load of brass and copper coils that somehow looked familiar.

Upon closer inspection, company executives realized the metal was the same shipment that had been hijacked from one of their own trucks the previous month.

According to the FBI, the coils had been resold four times before coming back to Dowling.

"To steal a junkyard is kind of difficult, but they did it," said Dr. Nick Onassis of Charlottesville, Virginia, after thieves had picked clean his 10-acre property of 30 tons of scrap. "I never saw a cleaner place."

I can't quite put my finger on this one. A masked bandit sidled into a convenience store in Santa Cruz, New Mexico, empty-handed and departed with all the money.

He simply pointed a forefinger, fluttered his thumb menacingly, and ordered the clerk to clean out the cash register.

"Are you serious?" asked the clerk.

"Yes," he replied—and got $250.

A run for the money. The Mercury Track and Racquet Shop in Toledo, Ohio, is not the store to pick for shoplifting if you plan a getaway on foot.

When a thief slipped out with a $15.98 gym bag, Tony Esposito, 31, the store owner, gave chase. After a few fast blocks, the thief huffed over his shoulder, "You can have your old bag," and tossed it aside.

Esposito, a jogger and former policeman, ignored the bait and kept up pursuit. Eventually the thief collapsed in a parking lot, exhausted. Esposito escorted him to the police station.

Apples, green beans, peanut butter, and baby powder may be hazardous to your health. Especially if they are in jars or cans . . . and especially if you're a thief.

A clerk in a clothing store in Superior, Wisconsin, threw an apple she'd been eating at a holdup man, hitting him in the chest. Startled, the bandit turned and fled.

A customer in a supermarket in Albany, New York, pitched a can of green beans at an armed robber, conking him in the left temple. Stunned, the robber released his female hostage and was disarmed by police.

Alberto Reyes, who worked in a store in Dallas, Texas, bombarded a would-be robber with jars of peanut butter till the hoodlum beat a retreat.

Tom Horne and Sam James, pharmacists in Bartlesville, Oklahoma, hurled cans of baby powder at a pair of thugs, who forthwith took a powder.

Deputy Sheriff Ted Gans thought he knew where to look for the $45,000 stolen from a café and home in Meridian, Mississippi.

For starters, he found $8,000 in $10 and $20 bills in the suspect's leg.

"I knew he had an artificial leg, and I knew there was a hole in it, and I knew him," said the sheriff.

A holdup man walked into a South Dakota liquor store and pointed his gun at clerk Veronica Taylor.

"This is a stickup. Give me everything in the register," he said.

Taylor told him there was no money in the register.

"I was just kidding. There are no bullets in the gun," the man replied and ran away.

Now watch this. A Sarasota, Florida, man who brought his watch into a local jewelry store for repairs was charged with grand theft. A clerk identified him as one of two men who had stolen $10,000 worth of diamond rings from the store earlier in the day.

Enrique Vargas Fernandez, 28, was captured as he held up a pedestrian in Mexico City while attired in his underwear.

Police said Fernandez always worked in his underwear so that if caught he could claim he had just been robbed himself.

Eddie McCartney, 37, got no respect when he charged into a jewelry store in Liverpool, England, and bawled, "This is a stickup!" Instead of cowering, everyone laughed. The owner chased him outside and straight into the arms of the law.

McCartney had neglected to remove the cork from the barrel of his toy gun.

A pistol-packin' stranger strode into a clothing store in Lafayette, Louisiana, handed a sack to the clerk, and commanded, "Fill 'er up!"

"With what?" asked the clerk.

The question struck the holdup man so funny that he howled with laughter and backed out of the store without stealing a cent.

1981

A burglar who ransacked a home in Pasadena, California, planned to make a clean getaway. He was arrested as he soaped himself in his victim's bathtub.

Stretching a point. Thieves had no difficulty in heisting nearly $1 million from an armored car parked outside a bakery in Providence, Rhode Island. The guards made a point of fixing rubber bands to the inside of the rear doors so that they didn't have to lock and unlock them each time they stopped for a pickup.

In Baton Rouge, Louisiana, a man pulled a gun on the cashier in a convenience store and barked, "Give it up!" Just then the pinball machine behind him uttered its recorded come-on: *"I want you to play me!"*

Startled pop-eyed, the would-be robber streaked out of the store.

CHAPTER 2

No Holds Barred

1969

Mrs. Houdini of the Hoosegow. Unhurriedly, Mrs. Susan Kimball took a screwdriver from her pocketbook and undid the 14 screws that held a window partition separating her from her husband in a California prison.

While nearly 100 curious prisoners and visitors looked on, Mrs. Kimball silently lifted out the window. Her husband squirmed through, and the couple walked serenely away.

At last, someone who does windows!

1971

A 38-year-old prisoner in Atlanta, Georgia, hanged himself with a shredded blanket, recovered, and was charged with the destruction of public property.

1978

Police seized Terry O'Brien, 46, as he climbed over the wall of the prison in Lewes, England. O'Brien, a homeless wanderer, stammered an explanation.

He had broken *into* the prison the previous night, seeking a quiet place to sleep. He was departing when "captured."

Using coin phones in an Alabama county jail, at least six inmates made $32,000 worth of illegal calls before being caught.

They favored long-distance chats, which they charged to fake credit cards or the telephone numbers of local citizens. The most popular number belonged to a 94-year-old woman, who got walloped with a bill for $1,800.

While imprisoned in a Utah county jail, William McGinley filed for the office of justice of the peace. He wasn't elected. Having forgotten to include the necessary fee, he didn't make the ballot.

Keith Phillips proved a serious pupil in the prison scaffolding course while serving time in Ackland, England. The lessons were all carefully taken down—as well as up and over. Using scaffoiding poles, he and another prisoner scaled a 16-foot fence and skedaddled.

But they couldn't stay above the law. Shortly after their escape, they were caught breaking into two houses.

1979

An inmate of a county jail in South Carolina dragged herself to the doctor with an unusual complaint. She had a bellyache from swallowing a hotel.

X rays revealed she had swallowed a hotel all right —while playing Monopoly. After treatment, she was returned to the sheriff's office with the note: *Go directly to Jail. Do not pass Go. Do not collect $200.*

Clarence R. Jones, 24, escaped from a work-release center in Birmingham, Alabama, but he didn't think his freedom would last long.

So he shopped around for a nice jail where prisoners were treated well and where they could smoke. After telephone calls to many jails, he decided upon one in Florida.

All his painstaking research did him no good. After spending less than eight hours in the prison of his choice, he was moved to another Florida county jail to await his return to Alabama.

That ain't no lady. . . .   Seventeen female volunteers in a tutoring program for inmates filed into an Oregon reformatory. Eighteen filed out.

Escapee Dan Burrows, 27, of Portland, was captured half an hour later as he was walking down a road. Reformatory officials were baffled as to where he obtained the woman's clothing and makeup.

Joe Kirkpatrick, 20, who had begun serving a sentence of 22 to 45 years, didn't ask any questions when he was suddenly released from a New Jersey prison.

Soon afterward he learned from a TV broadcast in Newark that he was wanted for escape. He turned himself in at the city's detention center.

After sorting out the mistake, the judge on the case remarked, "You can't blame him. He was told he could go, and he went."

Rachel Edmonds, 25, of England, "felt murderous" toward her boyfriend. So the safest place for her, she realized, was in jail.

But getting locked up wasn't easy.

She tried eating in restaurants and refusing to pay her bill. At one restaurant the employees took up a collection for her. At another, the customers did.

She rode in taxis and would not pay the fare. The drivers told her to be gone. She threw a milk crate at a window. The glass didn't break.

In desperation she took a taxi to the West End Central Police Station, waved a blank-firing starter's pistol at the driver, and ordered him to summon the police.

She finally got her wish: a year in jail.

Daniel Dobbs, 31, of Kamloops, British Columbia, had a different reason for wanting to stay a spell in the clink.

He needed a good place to write a book.

So he stole two cartons of cigarettes.

After nearly a month behind bars, Dobbs showed his writing to the judge.

"I commend you for your work," the judge said, and set the budding author free.

Now that was the write way.

1980

Jail-order catalog. Eric Farber, an inmate in a Connecticut prison, sued the warden and hobby manager because a hobby kit he had ordered by mail was lost after reaching the prison. He won.

Stuck on him. A woman who visited her husband in Birmingham Prison, England, smeared a wonder glue on her palm and his shortly before they shook good-bye. She was sent home "after several hours," the time surgeons needed to part the couple.

Shucks, it was playtime. Five men kicked out a fourth-floor window in a Nebraska prison break and slid to the outside world on bed sheets. Three were recaptured—two of them while playing on swings at a local park.

James Hoag escaped from an outside work detail at a West Virginia correctional institution on the warden's ten-speed bicycle.

Steel yourself for this one. Two convicts escaped from a Kansas prison by cutting through steel bars with dental floss dusted with tooth powder.

The warden promptly put dental floss on the prison's no-no list.

The $350,000 12-prisoner jail in a western state was termed the latest in modern criminology when it opened in 1974. Four years later so many prisoners had escaped that the county commissioner admitted, "I don't even want to go to town because when I'm seen, I'm laughed at and ridiculed."

HEH HEH

Trying to squeeze through a 6¼-by-13½-inch gap in the bars of his cell in a Colorado jail, Ralph Lee Johnson, 29, trapped himself, half in and half out. He had to be cut free with a hacksaw.

"He said he was trying to get his cigarettes," deadpanned an officer.

Two Maryland prisoners bid for freedom by laboriously inching their way along a ventilator shaft. They dropped down a few vents too soon—and landed in a detective's office.

If you can keep your head
when all about you. . . .   Left unguarded in a
holding cubicle in a midwestern city hall, a burglary
suspect sought to escape by climbing into the false
ceiling.

His noisy movements attracted a host of spectators.
They swapped guesses as to where he'd come down.

He finally descended on a ladder provided for him.

Throwing up his hands, he announced, "I'm the
maintenance man. Boy, do you have bugs up there!"

Jailed for drunken driving, a Lexington, Kentucky,
woman used her one telephone call to summon her
attorney. He stumbled into the police station "too in-
toxicated to be driving anyone home," according to
the station captain, and was locked in the cooler till
he sobered up.

CHAPTER 3

Wheel Crimes

1972

That dwedful wabbit!   Object of a police dragnet in Carter County, Tennessee, was a man who dressed up in a bunny suit and hurled hatchets at the windows of empty cars.

Blindman's buff. Police in Mississippi pulled over a car that had been zigzagging crazily through traffic. The driver was blind and had been taking directions from his passenger, who confessed he was too drunk to drive himself.

1977

A 9-year-old girl entered a Florida police station and politely asked if she could use the telephone. She had to call a taxi, she explained, because her purchases were too heavy to carry home on her bike.

A suspicious officer peeked outside. The $350 in "purchases" had just been stolen from a nearby store.

A Belgian motorist, driving the highway from Leuven to Liège, picked up a hitchhiker. Later a policeman stopped him for whizzing along at 81 mph. The officer wrote out a ticket, cautioned him to drive more slowly, and sent him on his way.

After a few miles the hitchhiker handed the driver the officer's ticket book with the comment: "Don't worry, you won't have any ticket. I just left jail. I'm a pickpocket."

1978

Take the bus and do the driving yourself. Darren Marcus, 13, of Los Angeles, claimed he merely wished to visit his aunt in New York City. Whatever his motive, he adopted the direct method.

He stole a 41-foot bus and drove it 200 miles before

being stopped by a roadblock across an interstate highway.

Authorities were amazed by the 4-foot 9-inch boy's ability to reach the pedals. They dubbed him "a classy driver."

He had maintained a steady 55 mph, waved to collectors as he sped through a bridge tollgate at 10 P.M., and manuevered down the twisting roads of the Donner Summit like a veteran.

His younger brother, Alan, 10, stole another bus at the same time and abandoned it in Pasadena.

When a midwestern city cracked down on scofflaws —people who owe fines—some of the worst offenders proved to be employed in City Hall!

Champ of champs was a 22-year-old secretary in the city budget office with 63 unpaid parking tickets totaling $1,555. An officer said he had written her another 22 tickets for failing to pay the original ones.

When her supervisor went to see about bailing her out of the clink, he learned he owed $346 in unpaid parking tickets himself.

Try car pooling.

Road test. A stolen car was left in Dobking, England, by a disgruntled thief who attached a note for the police: *This motor is totally unsafe. The owner should be prosecuted.*

A New Orleans man was held for destroying city property after denting a police car with his head.

Nailed in the act. Sabar Dolok Pasaribu, owner of a tire repair shop in Jakarta, Indonesia, received a 7-month jail sentence for his sharp business practices.

He admitted scattering nails on the street near his shop in the hope that punctured tires would be brought to him for repairs.

Some irate motorist shot and killed the only parking meter in Owyhee County, Idaho.

Rest in pieces.

Say cheese! In New York City thieves stole a tractor-trailer rig loaded with 40,000 pounds of mozzarella cheese. That's enough to supply the average pizza parlor for more than a year.

Oh, doze crooks. The driver of a stolen getaway car in Chicago played it so cool that he fell asleep on the job. After his two accomplices had robbed a gas station and tied up attendant Michael Skolka, they found their driver snoozing behind the wheel. Shaken awake, he panicked and ran off. All three were captured.

A bandit with flair hired a chauffeur-driven Cadillac limousine to take him on a one-night robbery spree in New York and New Jersey. He was arrested after holding up a drugstore and two motels.

The chauffeur told police he saw nothing suspicious in his client's uncommon route. "There are plenty of crazy people who hire limousines just to drive around and look at things."

The man who stole an electric organ from a church in Monterey, California, helped police load it into a truck for the trip back.

In Buffalo, New York, a 51-year-old man entered a police garage and drove off in an unmarked squad car. A few days later he exchanged it for a later model. As he was being arrested, he demanded $1.75, the price of the quart of oil he put into the second car.

She'll go no more a-roving. Two men robbed a convenience store while their female companion remained in the getaway car—or should have. When the men raced out to the car, they found it empty. The woman had waltzed to the rest room, taking the keys with her.

Police rounded up the trio and recovered all but three dollars of the $150 stolen.

Foiled in her attempt to rob a drugstore in Boise, Idaho, Louise Ryan, 25, sprinted outside and looked wildly about for means of getting away.

She hopped into a parked car, apparently mistaking the police markings for those of a taxi. Before she could order the driver to drive, the driver drove—to the station house.

A hair coiler.   Crooks in Las Vegas who stole a white-and-blue sport sedan got a worse shock than the car's owner. A pet boa constrictor was coiled in the backseat.

To date there has been no word—or screams—from the car thieves.

The old no-hands trick. A driver involved in an automobile collision in Chicago was handcuffed with his hands behind his back and put in the rear seat of a state trooper's car. While the trooper was off questioning others concerned in the accident, the prisoner wormed into the front seat and drove off—hands still shackled behind him.

A man and woman stuck up a drugstore in Honolulu and got $500—but they didn't get far. A block from the store their car ran out of gas. They were arrested, on foot.

1980

A Boulder, Colorado, man went to the top of a nearby mountain, put on his roller skates, and proceeded to sizzle down 3 miles of steep highway at 45 mph. Police ticketed him for speeding and running a stop sign.

Well, at least he didn't run out of gas.

Gary Fraser, 4, was in the living room of his home in Duluth, Minnesota, when he spotted someone stealing his bicycle. Jumping into the family car, he sped off in hot pursuit.

Since he had to stand on the seat to see through the windshield, he couldn't reach the brakes. The car ran a stop sign, plowed through some bushes, and ended up on a front porch.

The Minnesota Highway Patrol released Gary into the custody of his parents.

And the bicycle thief? He was Gary's older brother, Neil, 6.

Indy 5. Todd Nicholson, 5, was picked up by police after driving his grandparents' car some 25 miles on a highway from Gouverneur to Canton in upstate New York. He had cruised around town before stopping on a Canton street.

He told police he'd been driving for a year and never had an accident. His folks said it was his first Sunday spin.

Four Wisconsin police cars, farmed out to a private repair shop to have the transmissions rebuilt, came back with bargain jobs—new transmissions at no extra cost. The hitch: The new transmissions were stolen property.

A western city ordered 8,000 square feet of sod for a park. Shortly after delivery, someone rolled up a truck, rolled up the sod, and rolled out.

Some folks keep doing what comes naturally, as in the case of a 26-year-old man from Fargo, North Dakota. Arrested on hit-and-run and reckless driving charges, he spent several days in jail. Half an hour after his release, he was arrested for breaking into a car in the jail's parking lot.

A young man admitted paying a $20 traffic court fine in Wyoming with a $22 bill. Instead of the portrait of Andrew Jackson, the touched-up photocopy pictured a cigar-smoking chap in a Panama hat. Cashiers refused to say if he got two dollars in change.

An unflappable bandit who had just held up a small grocery store in Detroit, Michigan, found himself stalled in the parking lot with a dead battery.

He returned to the store and instructed the clerk to fetch jumper cables. Starting up his car, he waved a friendly thank-you and drove off.

A battery was lifted from a car outside the home of a couple in St. Paul, Minnesota. Stuck under a windshield wiper was the note: *We apologize for taking your battery, but our car stalled early this morning in front of your house. We will return it soon. Thank you.*

Sure enough, the battery appeared on the couple's doorstep a few days later, along with two tickets to the next Viking home football game, and another note of thanks.

Filled with renewed faith in the human race, the couple went off to the game. When they returned home, they found the house had been cleaned of all their valuables.

A locksmith rescued a 22-year-old man who reported losing the keys to an expensive sports car parked at the Pensacola, Florida, Airport.

With a set of newly made keys, the young man drove off spouting his undying gratitude.

Four days later the car's real owner showed up.

1981

The height of embarrassment. Taffy Thomas, 28, a jockey who stands 4 feet 11¾ inches, was driving to work at the Lingfield Race Track in Harlow, England. Police flagged him down on the expressway north of London.

The authorities thought that Thomas and his three passengers, also jockeys, were kids out joyriding in a stolen car. The quartet spent a brief time in jail before the mistake was straightened out.

A security guard at a truck-tractor terminal in Richmond, Virginia, declared he was not a thief. He told detectives that he had merely borrowed a tractor in order to drive to Norfolk to visit his girlfriend.

CHAPTER 4

Pet-ty Crimes

1978

Gary Hollamby, 12, went fishing near his hometown of Bedford, England. He didn't catch a fish. But he hooked a silver bowl that led him to $6,000 worth of silver thrown into the water by harried thieves.

A poodle named Puddins was the only occupant of a car left running in front of a bar in Horicon, Wisconsin. The car backed down the main street, jumped a curb, and crashed into a restaurant. Since Puddins didn't have a driver's license, police used a paw print for identification on the accident report.

A malcontented wine company employee dumped $600,000 of fine Burgundy into the sewers of Dijon, France, poisoning thousands of fish.

1979

Andy Potter, a mechanic, of Baring, England, had this problem: Money kept disappearing from his wallet when he left it at home.

Potter eventually solved the case. His dog, Pride, was bolting down the bills.

"I know we all have a taste for cash," declared Potter. "But this is ridiculous."

1980

Being a city dweller all his life, Artie Lloyd wasn't prepared to have a cow attack him.

Lloyd, 56, was working on the farm at an upstate New York correctional facility when it happened. A frisky, 500-pound Holstein reared up and struck him on the shoulders and neck with her front hooves.

Lloyd sued the state for failing to train him in the care and handling of cows, and for placing him in a dangerous situation.

The judge awarded him $52,000 for his injuries.

A Doberman pinscher snatched a purse containing $270 from Mrs. Janet Gorska, 24, wife of a Chicago policeman. The thief, wearing only a spiked collar, raced away with the purse in its jaws.

"What do we do for a lineup if we find a suspect?" asked a detective. "Do we have to have all Dobermans? Can't we throw in some cocker spaniels?"

Chip off the old block. Five years after a police dog named Dutch helped capture Sam Brower during a burglary, Dutch's son, Crow, tracked down Brower after he'd escaped from a federal halfway house in Dallas, Texas.

One of four burglary suspects in Ontario, California, tried to elude the police by hiding in a doghouse.

Pretty snakey.   A snake may not be a gun, but it sure is a weapon, and so the Chicago police called it armed robbery. The victim, Antonio Restrepo, 28, agreed.

A 15-year-old robber got into Restrepo's apartment, pointed a 6-foot boa constrictor at Restrepo's face, and hissed, "Give me all your money."

Rather than have the squeeze put on him, Restrepo handed over six dollars. The intruder rode off on a bicycle with his accomplice coiled around his neck.

Really bugged. A San Francisco jewelry store was broken into so often the owner put on a night watchman. The new employee was announced by a sign: WARNING! THIS AREA IS PATROLLED BY A TARANTULA. There hasn't been a break-in since.

CHAPTER 5

Hanky-Banky

1970

Open and shut case. Raymond Burles, an ultra-tidy French bank robber, took $6,400 at gunpoint and was nabbed on the spot. He had neatly packed the loot—and then his pistol—in a carrying case, and zipped it shut.

1974

What's in a name? A pair of New York City teen-age girls mugged a woman, got only four dollars, and indignantly demanded a check for their troubles. The woman suggested making it out to Cash.

Oh, no, the muggers were too smart for any of that tricky banking stuff. They insisted the woman write the check to the name of one of them. She did. The police did the rest.

1975

The impossible dream. A holdup man slipped a note to a teller in a Queens, New York, bank, demanding he be given *your tens, twenties, and thirties.*

1978

The mother of a 17-year-old youth admitted driving him to and from Dover, New Hampshire, where he was accused of holding up a bank. She explained to police that he had asked for the ride to the bank in order to withdraw money to buy a car of his own.

Police not only found the fingerprints of one of the two men who robbed a New Jersey bank of $3,204. They also found his finger.

A sawed-off shotgun carried by one of the robbers, Larry Collins, 22, accidentally discharged and struck him in the gloved hand. He pulled off the glove and threw it on the floor—with the tip of his left index finger inside it.

Police used the severed fingertip to run a fingerprint check that eventually brought Collins to justice.

On trial for robbing a bank in Fresno, California, a 19-year-old youth offered a far-out defense.

He needed cash, he said, to benefit mankind. He intended to invest in outer space colonies where earthlings could live happily, safe from pollution and overpopulation.

Two masked men—one armed with a pistol—jumped over a counter and dashed into the vault of a bank in Massachusetts. All they found was a bag of coins.

Figuring it wasn't worth the effort, the pair left the coins behind and fled in disgust.

Insulted at being termed a "two-bit crook" when he was arrested for burglarizing a luncheonette, Howard Moody, 38, of The Bronx, New York, ticked off twenty New York banks that he had robbed of a total of $78,000.

During a wave of holdups in the city, Banco de Ponce, New York's largest Puerto Rican bank, posted a sign reading:

> **Attention would-be robbers.**
> **This is a Spanish-speaking bank.**
> **If you intend to rob us, please be patient,**
> **for we might need an interpreter.**
> **Thank you.**
> ***The Management.***

And while you're waiting, would you mind getting me a cream soda?

In Tokyo, Japan, a high school student, 15, slipped from class for an hour. Upon his return, he showed a classmate a million yen ($50,000), a knife, and a model gun.

"I just robbed a bank," he whispered.

And to the police he explained, "I lost interest in school life. The bank robbery was the best way to be expelled."

Roberta Kirby, manager of an Indiana bank, succeeded in tripping the alarm before she was forced to the floor by four armed robbers.

During the course of the robbery, in which $63,000 was taken, the telephone kept ringing. Turned out to be the dispatcher at the county sheriff's office. He just wanted to tell the bank officers that their alarm was ringing.

Don't bank on it. A pistol-wielding desperado knocked over a bank in Los Angeles. As he hastened out with nearly $5,000, he dropped his wallet.

An hour later he trudged into police headquarters and surrendered the money and the toy gun he'd used. He said he realized where he must have lost his wallet and wanted to forget the whole thing.

The police said no deal.

1980

Still is sitting, still is sitting. . . . Police and FBI agents descended on a barber shop in The Bronx, New

York, and carted off the barber for bank robbery, leaving a shocked customer sitting in the chair with half his hair cut.

Ron Schatz filled out a withdrawal slip for $50 at a Rhode Island bank. It was no big deal—until he found himself about to be arrested for bank robbery.

The teller had touched a quiet alarm after reading what was written on the back of Schatz's slip: *This is a holdup.*

The police ironed it out. Schatz was the innocent victim of some practical joker who had written holdup messages in a stack of bank slips.

A promise is a promise. Officer Mitchell Stokes was sitting in his police car in Wilmington, Delaware, when a man sauntered up to him and declared he was "going across the street to rob the bank."

Stokes grinned, thinking it was a joke. "I'll be outside waiting to arrest you," he quipped back.

A few minutes later, Stokes was astonished to see the man, good as his word, coming out of the bank carrying his loot.

Good as his word, Stokes arrested him.

Keeping down overhead.   In Salt Lake City, Utah, a man held up a bank with an 18-inch stick. He escaped on a bicycle.

A bandit who threatened a teller with a banana that he held in his pocket like a gun got away with $726 from a bank in Santa Cruz.

Police overtook him five minutes later as he tried to make a telephone call from a pay booth. The banana was held as evidence.

The man who held up a bank in Brooklyn, New York, didn't know when to quit. He had stuffed $483,100 in small bills into two plastic garbage bags before he realized the load was too heavy to carry out.

Undaunted, he dragged the bags toward a side door. There one overtaxed bag split open. As he greedily gathered up the loose bills, the bank guards pounced on him.

A sportily dressed man went up to a bank teller in Albuquerque, New Mexico, and gave her the standard: "Give me all your money."

"Give you all our money?" the teller gasped. With that she trembled, swayed, and fell in a swoon.

The spectacle so surprised the bandit that he panicked and scurried off without a cent.

Then there is the case of the *holdup man* who fainted.

The teller at a Chicago bank accidentally tore the envelope as she was filling it with bills and coins. She told the nervous robber she'd get a sturdy cloth bag.

The strain of waiting proved too much. He had passed out and was lying on the floor when she returned with the bag.

Police in Kirksville, Missouri, rushed to a local bank to halt a robbery in progress only to find the robber sitting at a table contentedly munching a hamburger. Bank employees had provided him with two hamburgers after he'd said he was hungry.

When a female officer approached to arrest him, he looked up and remarked, "Just a minute, honey. Let me finish."

The police allowed him to eat the second hamburger on the ride to jail.

Definitely not an eat-and-run man.

Police arrested a 25-year-old man after he returned to the bank he had just robbed in Columbia, South Carolina. A tear gas bomb, planted in the sack with the money, exploded after he'd gone outside. Infuriated, he ran back into the bank complaining that his money was "catching fire."

The blond man pushed a note at the teller in a bank in Oakland, California. It read: *Put money in bag.*

"Is there any particular reason why I should?" inquired the teller.

"If you don't, I'll walk out the door," threatened the man.

"Go ahead," retorted the teller. "Be my guest."

Utterly confused, the would-be robber made a fast exit.

Nothin' here but us birds, boss.   A robber went out on a limb after stealing $1,500 from a bank in Riverhead, New York. Unable to start his car, he sprinted into a nearby wood. Police found him perched in a tree.

Must have been a branch bank.

A bandit who held up a bank in Waltham, Massachusetts, for $3,000 felt so flush that he telephoned for a taxi to take him home. Police captured him as he sat nonchalantly in the lobby of the bank waiting for his getaway ride.

1981

A mysterious, repentant thief slipped $290 in worn bills under the door of an auto dealer in Miami, Oklahoma. With the cash was a note: *I stole a set of hubcaps from a 1979 Monte Carlo. Here is the money I owe you. I am a born-again Christian, and I am trying to pay back my debts.*

Warren Croll, the auto dealer, didn't recall losing the hubcaps. He thought the thief might have made amends to the wrong place.

"If he did steal them from here, I couldn't tell you if they were mine or a customer's," Croll said.

CHAPTER 6

Odds and End

GRR-R-R

1970

A man on all fours attacked a female shopper in an Atlanta department store. He bit her first on the left ankle, then on the right ankle, then dashed away barking.

1973

A New York City man was flattened and sat upon by a woman he had tried to mug. In a fury of humiliation, he hurled his glass eye at the arresting officers.

1976

John King of Pensacola, Florida, was shot five times in the head at close range with a .22-caliber pistol following a dispute in a bar. None of the bullets pierced his skull.

"My ears are still ringing," he said. "Those shots were really loud."

1977

No butts about it.   A state supreme court ruled that the bullet taken from the behind of Dexter Collingsgood should not have been used as evidence to convict him.

The removal of the bullet, asserted the court, constituted illegal search and seizure, and the court ordered Collingsgood retried.

1978

No business like show business.   "I knew that when I used my real name and people saw me, I would be recognized, but I didn't think it would be this soon," said escaped prisoner Tommy Gerard, 26, about his appearance on a television game show.

A former correctional worker spotted him on the

TV screen. Gerard gave himself up when he learned the search was on.

"It was kind of stupid of me to leave," he said. He had only four months to serve on a one-year sentence in Danbury, Connecticut.

The urge to be in show business obviously had overcome caution. He had also taped two performances on another game show.

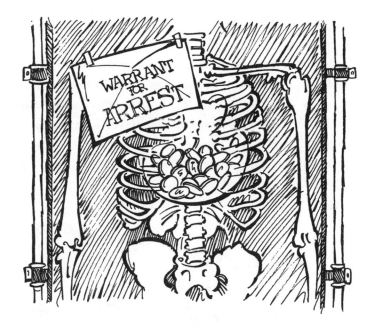

Sometimes you have to swallow hard. George Watts, 43, of England, found a way of being taken good care of. He made a habit of swallowing 50-pence coins and then going to the hospital.

A fishmarket ice porter, Watts enjoyed the sympathy and attention of the nurses so much that he hospitalized himself across the country. He was admitted complaining of chest pains, the natural result of swallowing coins.

The government, which paid his bills to the tune of $76 a day, finally got fed up, even if Watts didn't. He was sentenced to a year in jail on charges of obtaining hospital treatment by deception.

Dave Roth, 46, of Vallejo, California, just wanted to mow the tall grass around his house.

His mower struck a rock, casting sparks that set the grass afire. Before the flames were put out a week later, they had destroyed 39 homes, two businesses, and burned out 11,500 acres—$10 million worth of damage all told.

Lawn-cutting was unlawful in the area at the time, owing to the danger of fire. Roth pleaded no contest to a misdemeanor, a minor criminal charge.

Cop in. Tyron Stark was surprised by an 18-year-old youth who barged into his first floor apartment in Miami Beach, Florida.

"You've got to help me," the youth pleaded. "The cops are looking for me."

Upon questioning, the youth admitted that he had just snatched a purse from a woman a block and a half away.

Policeman Stark then and there showed his badge and his gun and arrested the panting intruder.

A 29-year-old man was arrested for trying to pass
$20 bills at the same Minneapolis restaurant two
nights in a row. Apparently he was color-blind as well
as persistent. The bills, produced on a copying machine, were black-and-white.

Normally Eileen Walsh's shoe store in Wichita, Kansas, accepts credit cards. The problem was that this woman customer paid for two pairs of shoes with a credit card that clearly wasn't hers.

The card belonged to Walsh. Her wallet full of credit cards had been stolen the month before.

"It was such a freak thing," she said afterward. "I was in shock."

So was the customer, who wound up in jail with time to rue her choice of shoe stores.

Umpire Bill Walters called a third strike during a baseball game in Greenwood, Mississippi. The batter's teammates promptly stormed from the dugout in protest. With equal promptness, Walters showed them who was boss. He pulled a gun.

Police arrested him and charged him with a misdemeanor. The charge was later upped to a felony when it was discovered Walters was an ex-convict out on probation.

The talk started, no one knows how: Mabel Callahan, 72, had $35,000 hidden in her small row house in Pittsburgh, Pennsylvania. The sum grew by word-of-mouth till the rumor had $45 million stashed under her floorboards.

In May the frightened old woman, who actually lived on a $247 monthly Social Security check, fled to a convent in order to escape a mob that was milling in front of her dwelling. One hundred police, on horseback and in riot gear, surrounded the house to keep out vandals.

"If there is no money in there, why are all these police guarding the place?" asked one suspicious teenager.

It took the police a full day, plus 19 arrests, to convince the doubters that Mabel Callahan's millions existed only in their heads.

1979

Edwin Parker, 20, of Washington, made up his mind to stop dodging the law. He tried to convince the officers at an Oregon police station that he was wanted for armed robbery. It took him five hours.

Hope Towsen wasn't certain whether she had housebreakers or elves on her hands.

For one week in December, persons unknown would enter her house by a window after she'd departed for work at a nearby car wash in Orlando, Florida.

Towsen, 18, told police that the intruders played cards, raided the refrigerator, and napped on her bed.

"Yesterday I came home and they'd walked my dog," she said. "Two days before, they had made cookies and washed the dishes."

They had washed, however, only what they had used. *Her* dirty breakfast dishes were left in the sink.

Next time call room service.

A 26-year-old New Orleans man was held on $37,500 bail after he was identified by five women who said he pulled a gun on them and forced each one to give him a kiss.

A 20-year-old man walked into an Indiana county jail to apply for a job as an ambulance driver. He was turned down for the job, but not for a cell.

Since the previous May, he had been wanted for burglary.

No luckier was a 22-year-old West Virginia man. He applied for a dispatcher's job at a police station.

When he returned to see how he'd made out, he was arrested. The police had found warrants charging him with two counts of the sale and transfer of marijuana.

A woman strode into a police station in upstate New York and threatened to shoot any officer asleep on the job. To back up her words, she produced a .357-magnum handgun, flashed it briefly, and strode out.

On-the-job training. Pete Olson, 26, of Kansas City, Missouri, wanted to work in a grocery store. He didn't think he could get a job merely by applying for it.

So he broke into the store and restocked a few shelves. Then he waited around for the doors to open so that he could show off his work to the owners.

He didn't get hired. What he got was a mistrial when the jury deadlocked at 9–3 in favor of clearing him of the charge of burglary.

Don't bother checking the pawn shops. James Wagner bought a house in Tulsa, Oklahoma. He planned to move it to his property in Muskogee.

Somebody beat him to it.

On July 2 he drove out to do some work on the old wood frame building. He stared at the foundation. The house was gone.

"You don't accidentally move a house," he said in disbelief. "You have to jack it up, and then it takes two or three days before you can get it onto the street."

Now that's what I call a housing shortage!

An Irish lifeguard named Francis Sullivan decided to get out of the swim and closer to the heart of things. He became an overnight surgeon.

The shortcut brought him into criminal court in London, England, where he pleaded guilty to charges of dishonestly obtaining medical credentials and pocketing $1,555 in fees between May and November, 1977.

During one 24-day span, the fake doctor performed 17 operations. He limited his surgery to arms, legs, hips, fingers, and an ankle.

According to a hospital source, his patients appeared to be "perfectly satisfactory."

Two brothers, 10 and 12, hid themselves in a San Francisco store after closing time and then went on an all-night binge in the toy department and at the soda fountain.

The next morning several dozen employees, aided by security guards and policemen, searched the store for 30 minutes before finding the brothers hiding under a pile of fabrics.

"It was a mess," one employee said. "The TVs were on, the toys were broken, and there was melted ice cream and strawberry syrup all over the floor. They'd been making sundaes."

Thirty-two policemen rushed to a wedding reception in San Mateo, California, to quell a free-for-all that began when the groom threw the wedding cake in the bride's face.

Hard day's night. In Levittown, New York, a startled homeowner found a 28-year-old burglar snoring on the sofa.

"It's all this night work," the burglar informed the police. "My body can't get used to it. All of a sudden, I felt so exhausted I just had to lie down."

1980

Roberta Summers, 47, of Bartow, Florida, was at the supermarket checkout counter when her pocketbook, in which she kept a gun for protection, fell to the floor. The gun discharged, wounding her in the forehead.

She ended up in the hospital's criminal ward after police arrested her for carrying a concealed weapon.

The naked truth. A woman accused of shoplifting in a discount store in Newport News, Virginia, dressed down employees who said she had stuffed a leather jacket under her skirt. Then she undressed to prove her innocence beyond the scantiest doubt.

Having satisfied the employees and a crowd of fascinated onlookers, she put her clothes back on and majestically swept out the door.

Nyet fair. Home from the summer Olympics in Russia, some New Yorkers discovered that the Russian 4-kopek coin, worth 5 cents, fit their city's subway turnstiles. Subway tokens at the time cost 60 cents.

A Minnesota man was accused of imprisoning a 36-year-old teacher, along with her 8-year-old daughter, in a closet for seven weeks before they escaped. His reason: He was still angry about the grade the teacher had given him in an algebra class 14 years before.

Tick, tick, chick. A terrified woman called police headquarters in Oakland, California, and reported a bomb ticking outside her front door.

A police officer rushed to the scene and discovered a chicken pecking on the porch.

"As a matter of fact, it did sound like a bomb," he said.

Open and claused case. Richard Bilby, 40, was fined $50 for his part in the annual Christmas parade in Toronto. Bilby shouted, "There is no Santa Claus," while supporting a sign that read, DOWN WITH SANTA.

New York City spent thousands of dollars to set up a program to teach young people the printing trade. The school was soon making money—its own.

A ring of counterfeiters that included at least one member of the faculty took over after classes. They turned out $50,000 in $5, $10, and $20 bills. The funny money received flunking grades.

"The paper was too thin, the color was too light, the details were missing," commented a special agent.

Two robbers left Judy Pace, 20, of Toronto, Canada, bound and gagged on her bed.

Wiggling to a push-button telephone, she toppled the receiver off the hook and pressed the "0" button with her nose. The operator, hearing her mumbling, called the police.

"Thank God for push-button phones," Pace said afterward. "I could never have done it with a dial phone. My nose isn't sharp enough."

Roar, lady, roar. Three Seattle patrol cars and a patrol supervisor responded to a 10:30 P.M. report that a woman in an apartment complex was screaming her head off.

Sure enough, a woman was screaming—at the television. On the screen was the last minute of the heart-stopping National Basketball Association game between the Seattle Supersonics and the Milwaukee Bucks. Her team, the Supersonics, won in the final seconds of overtime.

Leonardo da Toenail. A young man crawled under library tables and painted the toenails of several University of Southern California coeds while they were studying.

Campus police were alerted by a coed who said she walked into the library with pink nails and walked out with green ones.

However, none of the young women filed formal complaints.

"I don't think they want to see the guy again," said a Los Angeles Police Department spokesman. "Besides, maybe they decided he'd done a good job."

Two pie-throwing pranksters smacked a Michigan State University instructor during a lecture, but the

joke was on them. The class was on closed circuit television, and their antics were caught on camera.

A 72-year-old woman in Austin, Texas, paid $800 to have her roof sprayed with a silver paint that supposedly patched leaks. The foreman of the crew told her that her husband had placed the order.

The job required a compressor, a hose, and all of ten minutes.

Afterward the woman told police that she knew the work was an out-and-out fake. Her husband had died a year ago.

But the foreman was so convincing, she explained.

What a line. Donna Paulding, 36, of Hackensack, New Jersey, pleaded guilty to wiretapping her boyfriend's home. She was caught when she got her wires crossed with authorities, who were also listening in on her boyfriend's conversations.

Until his capture, Richard Carr, a hardware store clerk in Florida, was known simply as the mysterious Dr. Upchuck. For more than a year he telephoned women hospital patients, and, posing as a doctor, advised them to "stick your finger down your throat and throw up."

An Arkansas man received the J. Edgar Hoover Public Service Award at the National Conference on Crime in Miami Beach, Florida. Back in his hotel room, he placed the silver plaque on the dresser. The next morning he awoke to find it had been stolen.

A man was arrested for ripping a sink from a bus station men's room in Knoxville, Tennessee. He insisted he was only trying to recover 50 cents that slipped down the drain.

Goo for him! Officials allowed Neraide Coimbra to be with her son Alexandre when they questioned him for two hours at the police station in Belo Horizonte, Brazil. Mrs. Coimbra denied neighbors' charges that Alexandre's crying disturbed them.

"He only cries when we take him out of the bathtub because he likes to play in the water all the time," she said.

Alexandre, 7 months old, was released. According to police, it was his first arrest.

The mayor of a large eastern city suspended eight of the city's tax collectors for failing to pay their own taxes on time.

A juvenile court judge appointed a lawyer to defend a penniless youth accused of armed robbery. The youth's mother objected.

The lawyer, she explained, "put me in jail twice when he was a judge, and I don't want him representing my son."

The judge appointed another lawyer.

1981

In Caracas, Venezuela, Anibal López felt the prick of a knife in his back. A voice growled, "Hands up!"

A moment later the attacker changed his mind and raced away as if chased by a horde of demons.

"I don't know what got into him. Maybe he recognized me," said López, who happened to be the national karate champion.

Book her. Lillian Hofbeck, 31, of Tennessee, spent five hours behind bars for failing to pay late fines of $122 on 13 overdue books from her county public library.

Bratwurst to go. A drunk staggered into a fast-food shop in Frankfurt, Germany, and yawped, "Your bratwurst or your life!"

He managed to escape with *his* life, but not before the employees had enthusiastically clobbered him.

No fish story, reel-ly. When Ann Kean stepped outside her parked camper in San Diego, California, she saw a fishing line leading from her door.

She followed the line down the street and around a corner. It led to the window of a parked station wagon. Inside was the end of the line, her fishing rod.

The unstrung thief was arrested by police, who found his car filled with articles stolen from other vehicles in the area.

Victor Frank, 20, was about to be tried for burglary in New York City when he pulled a classic escape. He strolled past the judge and two cops and out the court-room door.

An alarm that was set off in the Vatican bank caused guards to activate the tiny city-state's sophisticated security system. Instantly visitors to the museums and offices as well as residents found themselves imprisoned behind locked doors.

But only for a few minutes. Investigation disclosed that the alarm had been set off accidentally—by a cleaner's feather duster.

Business as Usual

"That's all," Encyclopedia said, closing his notebook. "The end."

Sally, Charlie, and Benny protested. They wanted to hear more.

"You have two other notebooks," Sally said. "Read them, too!"

"Some other day," Encyclopedia replied. "The rain has stopped."

"It's too wet to play ball," Benny said.

"And too early to go home for dinner," Charlie observed. "Hey—Hymie!"

Hymie Goodman had entered the detective agency. He marched straight to Encyclopedia and exclaimed, "Someone kidnapped Max."

"Who's Max?" inquired Encyclopedia.

"My parrot," answered Hymie. "He's no ordinary parrot. How many birds do you know that can sing 'Frosty, the Snowman' in Yiddish?"

"Golly," Sally said. "What a talent."

"Describe Max, please," requested Encyclopedia.

"He has a yellow head and a green body with red shoulders," Hymie said. "He's flat-footed, and he likes to talk to dogs."

Benny and Charlie made quietly for the door. They waved good-bye to the detectives.

Hymie took a quarter from his pocket. He placed it on the gas can beside Encyclopedia.

"I want to hire you," Hymie said. "Find Max. Gosh, he must be scared out of his feathers. He's probably wondering what is happening."

"Now don't worry," Encyclopedia said. "We'll find him."

It was business as usual again in the Brown Detective Agency.

About the Author

Author DONALD J. SOBOL says: "This book developed out of years of writing mystery fiction and represents three years of collecting oddities full-time from the world of real crimes. The stories are all true, but when I recounted them to friends during the course of writing, no one believed me."

Mr. Sobol is the author of the highly acclaimed Encyclopedia Brown books. His awards for these books include the Pacific Northwest Reader's Choice Award for *Encyclopedia Brown Keeps the Peace* and a special Edgar from the Mystery Writers of America for his contribution to mystery writing in the United States.

Donald Sobol is married and has four children. A native of New York, he now lives in Florida.

Ms. Joni Is a Phony!

Pictures by
Jim Paillot

Dan Gutman

HARPER
An Imprint of HarperCollinsPublishers

To Toby Katz

My Weirdest School #7: Ms. Joni Is a Phony!
Text copyright © 2017 by Dan Gutman
Illustrations copyright © 2017 by Jim Paillot

Library of Congress Control Number: 2016935897
ISBN 978-0-06-242929-2 (pbk. bdg.)–ISBN 978-0-06-242931-5 (library bdg.)

Typography by Kathleen Duncan
16 17 18 19 20   CG/LSCH   10 9 8 7 6 5 4 3 2 1
❖
First Edition

Contents

Zombie-Free Zone

My name is A.J. and I hate zombies.

Zombies are dead people who come back to life. That's weird.

I've never seen a zombie in the real world. But after I go to sleep, my dad watches this TV show about zombies, and one night I sneaked over to the top of the stairs to watch. It was scary!

After that I was sure there was a family of zombies living in my bedroom closet. I told my dad, and he got out the vacuum cleaner and used it to suck up all the zombies that were living in my closet. It was like *Ghostbusters*. But I'm not going to use my closet anymore, just to be on the safe side. And I'm *never* going to use the vacuum cleaner, because there's a family of zombies living inside it.

Don't worry. There's nothing else about zombies in this book. Don't you hate it when you're reading a book and they start talking about stuff that has nothing to do with the book?*

Anyway, it was Friday, my third favorite

---

*Ha-ha, made you look! The story is up there, dumbhead!

day of the week. Why is Friday my third favorite day of the week? Because on Friday, there's no school tomorrow!

My teacher, Mr. Cooper, came flying into the room. Mr. Cooper thinks he's a superhero. But he's not a very good one, because he slipped on a sheet of paper and almost slammed his head into the cloakroom door. Mr. Cooper was carrying

an armful of papers, and they scattered all over the place when he fell.

"Guess what?" Mr. Cooper asked.

"Your butt?" said Michael, who never ties his shoes.

"You ate a cashew nut?" said Ryan, who will eat anything, even stuff that isn't food.

"You got a crew cut?" said Alexia, this girl who rides a skateboard all the time.

"You went to Pizza Hut?" said Neil, who we call the nude kid even though he wears clothes.

Any time somebody asks "Guess what?" you should always answer with obnoxious rhymes. That's the first rule of being a kid.

4

"No," said Mr. Cooper. "Monday will be Picture Day! Everybody take one of these forms and bring it home to your mom or dad to fill out."

"*Eeek!* Picture Day?" yelled Andrea Young, this annoying girl with curly brown hair. "I *love* Picture Day!"

"Me too!" said Emily, who always loves everything that Andrea loves.

"We have to draw pictures?" I asked. "What's the big deal? We draw pictures all the time."

"No, dumbhead!" Andrea told me, rolling her eyes. "Picture Day is when a photographer comes to school and takes our picture for the yearbook."

I was going to say something mean to

Andrea, but she and the girls were jumping up and down and freaking out about Picture Day.

"What are you going to wear?"

"What are you going to wear?"

"What are you going to wear?"

In case you were wondering, all the girls were asking what they were going to wear.

Ugh. Girls are always worried about what they're going to wear. If you're a girl and you're reading this, let me give you a clue—nobody cares what you wear! You could all wear laundry bags over your heads and I wouldn't notice.

Come to think of it, it would be cool if

all the girls came to school wearing laundry bags over their heads.

"I'm going to wear my new blue dress!" said Andrea.

"I'm going to wear *my* new blue dress too," said Emily, who always does everything Andrea does.

Ugh. I'm going to wear whatever is on the top of my drawer.

"I'm going to wear my new shades," said Ryan.

"Why would you take the shades off your windows?" I asked.

It would be weird to wear window shades.

"Not *those* kinds of shades, dumbhead!" said Ryan. "Shades are sunglasses."

"Oh, I knew that," I lied. "Why are you going to wear shades on Picture Day?"

"Because shades look cool," Ryan told me. "Secret agents always wear shades. I want to look like a secret agent in the yearbook."

Ryan is weird.

I hate Picture Day. Do you want to know the thing I hate the *most* about Picture Day?

I'm not going to tell you.

Okay, okay, I'll tell you.

But you have to read the next chapter. So nah-nah-nah boo-boo on you.*

---

*Hey, how come this book is called *Ms. Joni Is a Phony!* when there's no character named Ms. Joni?

The Torture Department

The thing I hate most about Picture Day is that my mom forces me to buy new clothes. Ugh, I hate shopping! And the worst kind of shopping is clothes shopping, because you have to spend hours trying on clothes.

I don't mind grocery shopping so much.

You don't have to try stuff on at the super-market. Like, you don't have to try on the bananas before you buy them. That would be weird.

"Let's *go*, A.J.!" my mom shouted up the stairs on Saturday morning. "We have to get you new clothes for Picture Day."

"What's wrong with my old clothes?" I hollered back.

"You'll have the picture for the rest of your life," my mom said. "That way you'll know what you looked like when you were in third grade. Don't you want to look nice for the picture?"

"No."

It isn't fair! I thought only the *girls* had

to care about looking nice. Boys should be allowed to look like slobs. That's the first rule of being a boy.

I could have begged and pleaded and cried and freaked out. Sometimes that works. But I knew there was no arguing with my mom. When your mom wants to go shopping, there's no stopping her. That's the first rule of being a mom.

We drove a million hundred miles to the department store. A department store is a store that has a lot of departments, so it has the perfect name.

My mom got a shopping cart. You know it's bad news when your mom gets a shopping cart, because that means she's planning to be shopping for a *long* time. Ugh. But shopping carts are cool, too, because it's fun to run around the department store pushing a cart and bumping into stuff.

We wheeled our cart past the furniture department.

We wheeled our cart past the kitchen department.

We wheeled our cart past the garden department.

Man, department stores have a *lot* of departments.

Finally, we got to the boys' department. Or as I call it, THE TORTURE DEPARTMENT. And you'll never believe what was in the boys' department.

Boys!

Well, of *course* there were boys in the boys' department. That's why it's called the boys' department! But the boys in the boys' department weren't just *any* boys. They were my friends Michael, Ryan, and Neil!

"What are *you* guys doing here?" I asked.

"The same thing *you're* doing here," grumbled Michael.

"We have to buy new clothes for Picture Day," grumbled Ryan.

"Bummer in the summer," grumbled Neil.

The guys were all with their mothers. None of our dads were there. I can't wait until I'm a dad so I won't have to go clothes shopping anymore.

Actually, my mom wanted my dad to come, but he said he would rather poke hot needles in his eyes than go clothes shopping. That was weird. I don't know why anybody would want to poke hot needles in their eyes.

Our moms were all gabbing about the weather and other boring stuff that grown-ups talk about. That's when this salesman came over. His name tag said "Mr. Bob."

"What can I do for you young men?" Mr. Bob asked us.

"You can close the store early so we can get out of here," I told him.

"Very funny, A.J.," said my mom. "Mr. Bob, these boys need new clothes for Picture Day."

"Aha! Picture Day! You boys came to the right place," said Mr. Bob. "What are your favorite colors?"

"Yellow," said Ryan and Neil.

"Plaid," said Michael.

"Orange," I said.

"These boys need plain dark pants, white shirts, dark jackets, and ties," said Ryan's mom.

Ties? Really? I *hate* ties! What's the deal with ties? Ties are dumb. The last time I wore a tie, I thought I was gonna choke.

Mr. Bob led us to a rack of boring-looking man clothes for boys. Then we had to go in the fitting room to try them on.

The fitting room is the only good thing about the torture department. They have a mirror in there that lets you see your-self from three sides, all at the same time. That is *cool.* And it's even cooler when you stick your face right next to the line where two mirrors meet.

"Hey look," I told the guys. "I have one eye in the middle of my head!"

We spent a million hundred hours try-ing on clothes. I thought I was gonna die. Mr. Bob had to keep running back and forth getting other clothes because our moms were never satisfied. Poor Mr. Bob. I can't believe he has to work in the torture department every day. Mr. Bob should get a medal, or a new job.

"Are you kids almost done in there?" shouted Michael's mom.

Finally, we all had on our new suits. Mr. Bob helped us tie our ties. We looked just like our dads, but shorter. So naturally, we had to play a game I call Pretend to Be Your Dad.

"Look, I'm Mr. Businessman," I told the guys as we looked in the mirror. "Give me your money."

"You're fired!" said Ryan. "Let's read the newspaper and go play golf."

"Nice weather we're having," said Michael. "I need some coffee."

"I'm a funeral director," said Neil. "After we bury the bodies, let's go watch the game."

Our moms were calling us, so we had to stop playing Pretend to Be Your Dad and come out of the fitting room. Mr. Bob lined us up, just like they do at the police station with bank robbers.

That's when the weirdest thing in the history of the world happened. Our moms burst out crying.

"Aren't they handsome?" blubbered my mom.

"They look so grown up!" blubbered Michael's mom.

Sheesh, get a grip! The moms were

sobbing and slobbering all over the place They started pulling tissues out of their purses and blowing their noses into them.

Well, they were blowing their noses into the *tissues*, not into their purses. It would be weird to blow your nose into a purse.

"I can't believe my baby Ryan looks so mature and grown-up," said Ryan's mom. "It seems like only yesterday that he was wearing diapers."

"You were wearing diapers yesterday?" I asked Ryan.

The moms took out their cell phones and started taking pictures of us. Do you know what a bunch of moms are called when they take pictures of you?

Mamarazzi! Get it?*

"Say 'cheese'!" my mom shouted.

Ugh. Why do you have to say "cheese" every time somebody takes your picture? What does cheese have to do with pictures? I don't even like cheese.

"Stop scowling, boys," said Mr. Bob. "Smile for the camera."

"You look *very* handsome, A.J.!" said my mom.

"I look terrible," I replied. "I hate getting my picture taken."

"Don't mind my son," Mom told Mr. Bob. "He *says* he hates everything."

"I understand," Mr. Bob replied. "I was a boy once."

---

*Mamarazzi? Paparazzi? That's what you call a joke!

"Just once?" I said. "I'm a boy *all* the time."

Mr. Bob is a nut job.

The mamarazzi took pictures of us from every possible angle. After a while, my face hurt from smiling.

Finally, we were finished in the torture department. My mom paid for the suit, and I pushed our shopping cart out to the parking lot. That's when I got the greatest idea in the history of the world.

"Hey Mom," I said. "Since you took all those pictures of me in my new suit, we don't need to take any pictures on Picture Day. So, can I stay home from school on Monday?"

"No!"

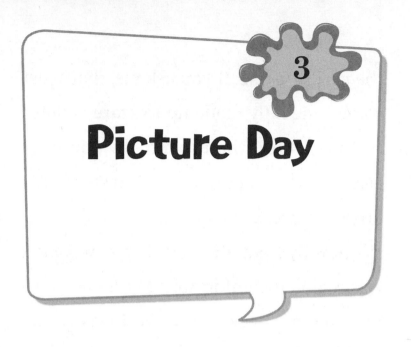

Picture Day

It was Monday. Picture Day. The worst day in the history of the world.

I know I said there aren't any zombies in this book, but did you ever hear about the Picture Day Zombie? My friend Billy, who lives around the corner, told me about it. The Picture Day Zombie is a zombie who only comes out on Picture Day, so he has the perfect name. If you ask me, that's just something Billy made up to scare people.

Don't worry, there won't be anything else about zombies for the rest of this book. I promise.

Anyway, I got dressed. My new jacket was really uncomfortable. My tie was cutting into my neck. I thought I was gonna die. My parents were in the kitchen drinking coffee and reading the newspaper, because that's what parents have to do. It's the law.

Before I could leave for school, they had to fill out the sheet of paper Mr. Cooper had given us. It was an order form so we could buy pictures.

"Package #1 is two eight-by-tens and two five-by-sevens," my mom told my dad. "Package #2 is three eight-by-tens and four five-by-sevens. And Package #3 is five eight-by-tens and six five-by-sevens. Which package should we buy, dear?"

"I couldn't care less," Dad replied.

My dad and me are a lot alike.

"The important thing, A.J.," he told me, "is to turn in this envelope and make sure you don't lose it. Money doesn't grow on trees, you know."

"Actually, it *does*," I told him. "Money is made out of paper, right? And paper is made out of trees. So money *does* grow on trees."

"Go to school now," said my dad.

Arguing with your parents is fun. That's the first rule of being a kid.

I took the envelope full of money and put it in my backpack. When I got to school, everybody was dressed up in their new Picture Day clothes.

"You look *very* handsome, Arlo!" said annoying Andrea, who calls me by my real name because she knows I don't like it.

"I do *not*," I told her.

"*Ooooo!*" Ryan said. "Andrea said A.J. looks handsome. They must be in *love!*"

"When are you gonna get married?" asked Michael.

Andrea had one of those rolling suit-cases with her. She opened it, and it was filled with mirrors, combs, hair spray, and all kinds of other junk girls use. Man, it sure takes a lot of stuff to make Andrea look good.

She started fussing with her hair. That's when the most amazing thing in the history of the world happened.

Emily walked into the room.

Well, that's not the amazing part. Emily walks into the room every day. The amazing part was that she was wearing a ski mask over her face!

There are only two reasons why you would wear a ski mask. The first reason is

29

because you're going skiing. The second reason is that you're going to rob a bank. Bank robbers always wear ski masks. I guess they like to go skiing after they

finish robbing a bank.

I knew Emily wasn't going skiing, and I was pretty sure she wasn't going to rob a bank either.

Everybody was looking at her.

"Don't look at me!" she shouted.

"What's wrong, Emily?" asked Mr. Cooper. "Are you okay?"

"I have . . . a pimple!"

Oh. I guess there are *three* reasons why you would wear a ski mask.

Emily started crying, as usual. She took off the ski mask. Her pimple was *tiny*. Nobody ever would have noticed it if she hadn't been wearing a ski mask. And I never would have looked at her if she hadn't told us not to look at her.

Emily is weird.

"Don't worry, Emily," Mr. Cooper told her. "That won't show up in your picture. They can Photoshop that pimple right off your face."

Emily stopped crying. We pledged the allegiance, and then an announcement came over the loudspeaker.

"All classes, please report to the playground."

"They're going to shoot the photo of the whole school!" said Andrea. "I'm so excited!"

We had to walk a million hundred miles to the playground. There were bleachers out there, and most of the classes were already on them. Our school has about five hundred kids.

Our class lined up across the back row of the bleachers. Ryan, Michael, and Neil were all the way on the right side. I had to stand between Emily and Andrea on the left side. Ugh.

Everybody was talking. Our principal, Mr. Klutz, came out. He has no hair at all. If we used hair instead of money, he would be broke. Mr. Klutz held up his hand and made a peace sign, which means "shut up." So we all stopped talking.

He told us that the photographer's name was Ms. Joni and that she would be here any minute.

That's when the most amazing thing in

the history of the world happened. There was a noise in the sky.

We all looked up.

A helicopter was flying around.

It was getting lower.

Then it landed in the middle of the playground!

And you'll never believe who got out of the helicopter.

No, I'm not going to make you wait until the next chapter to find out. I'll tell you right now.

It was Ms. Joni!*

---

*It's about time she showed up!

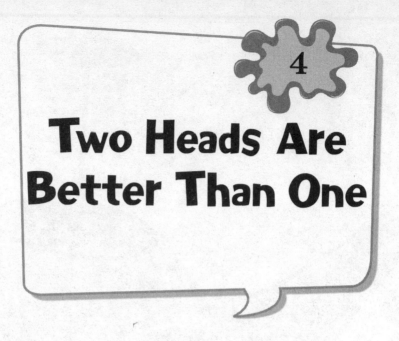

Two Heads Are Better Than One

Ms. Joni was really tall and skinny. She went over and hugged Mr. Klutz like they were old friends.

"Ms. Joni and I are old friends," Mr. Klutz told us. "We went to college together, and then she went on to become a famous photographer. Her pictures are in all the fashion magazines. It was so nice of her to come here to take pictures of you kids for Picture Day."

We gave Ms. Joni a standing ovation. It *had* to be a standing ovation, because we were all standing.

"Well, hello and thank you!" Ms. Joni said. "It is simply *fabulous* to be here. You all look *fabulous*. And this is a *fabulous* school. I bet my old friend Mr. Klutz is a *fabulous* principal."

Man, Ms. Joni sure says "fabulous" a lot. Just about every other word from her mouth was "fabulous."

"Blah blah fabulous blah blah fabulous blah blah fabulous blah blah fabulous blah blah," said Ms. Joni.

See what I mean?

"Ms. Joni is really *famous!*" Andrea whispered in my ear. "She takes pictures of all the supermodels."

"Models have superpowers?" I said. "That is *cool.*"

I wondered which superpowers models have. It would be cool to have superheat vision. Then you wouldn't need a microwave oven. You could just heat up your food by looking at it.

"Supermodels don't have superpowers, dumbhead!" Andrea told me. "They're the most famous models in the world."

"I knew that," I lied.

What is Andrea's problem? Why can't a truck full of microwave ovens fall on her head?

"I bet *you* could be a supermodel, Andrea," whispered Emily.

"People *do* tell me I have nice cheekbones," Andrea whispered back.

Cheekbones? What?! Cheeks have bones? That's a new one on me. I felt my cheeks. They were all skin. I don't have bones in my cheeks. How would you be able to eat if you had bones in your cheeks? Gross! The whole idea of cheekbones made me want to throw up.

Ms. Joni set up a big camera on a tripod. She told us it was a special camera that would slowly move from left to right as it was taking the picture so it could get all five hundred of us in the shot. We would have to stay perfectly still for five seconds while the camera moved across all our faces.

"Okay," said Ms. Joni. "When I say 'smile,' everybody stay still for five seconds. Ready?"

"Ready!" we all said.

That's when I got the greatest idea in

the history of the world.

"Smile!" said Ms. Joni.

The camera was pointing at my side of the bleachers. As soon as it started moving, I jumped down off the back of the bleachers.

"One . . . ," said Ms. Joni.

I landed on the grass behind the right bleachers.

"Two . . . ," said Ms. Joni.

I ran across the back of the bleachers to the other side, where my friends were.

"Three . . . ," said Ms. Joni.

I climbed up the back of the bleachers.

"Four . . . ," said Ms. Joni.

I stood up between Ryan and Michael.

"Five . . . ," said Ms. Joni.

The camera was pointing right at my side of the bleachers.

"Fabulous!" said Ms. Joni. "Nice job standing still, everybody."

"A.J., what are *you* doing here?" Ryan whispered in my ear right after the picture was finished.

"I jumped down from the other side of the bleachers after the camera took my picture over there," I explained. "Then I ran over here."

"Why did you do that?" asked Michael.

"So I could be in the picture twice!" I told them. "Two heads are better than one!"

"A.J., you're a genius!" said Ryan.

I should get the Nobel Prize for that idea. That's a prize they give out to people who don't have bells.

Fabulo

After Ms. Joni took the school picture, we had to go back to our classroom and wait to be called for our class picture. Mr. Cooper said we could sit at our desks and talk to each other as long as we used our inside voices.

That makes no sense at all. My voice is

the same wherever I am.

I took a sheet of paper from my desk and drew a picture of a rocket ship. Alexia read a book on skateboarding. Andrea and Emily took mirrors out of Andrea's suitcase and started fussing with their hair.

"Maybe Ms. Joni will notice me," Andrea whispered as she put some girly gunk on her face. "It would be exciting to be a model."

Ugh. I really wanted to say something mean about Andrea's face, but it's hard to say mean stuff with an inside voice.

Finally, after we sat there for a million hundred hours, an announcement came over the loudspeaker.

"Attention, Mr. Cooper's class. Please report to the gym to have your class picture taken."

We lined up in size order and walked to the gym. A plain white background was on the wall in the corner, and there were seats in front of it for the class to sit on. Ms. Joni had two big umbrellas set on either side. That was weird.

"Do you think it's going to rain inside the gym?" Ryan asked her.

"No, silly!" said Ms. Joni. "The umbrellas are here to bounce the lights on you and make you look fabulous."

Ms. Joni told us to sit down. There was a sign that said MR. COOPER'S THIRD-GRADE CLASS. We had to sit boy-girl-boy-girl so we couldn't sit next to anybody we liked. Mr. Cooper stood next to the class.

"This is going to be fabulous!" said Ms. Joni. "Are you kids ready?"

"Yes!" said all the girls.

"No!" said all the boys.

Ms. Joni pushed a button, and a big

flash went off. The light bounced off the umbrellas.

Snap!

"That's fabulous!" Ms. Joni said. "Now tilt your heads to the right."

Snap!

"A little to the left."

Snap!

"Chins up."

Snap!

"Not that far. Don't squint."

Snap!

"Keep your cheeks down."

Snap!

"Hands to your sides."

Snap!

"Cross your feet at the ankles."

Snap!

"Look at me."

Snap!

"Now look over my head."

Snap!

"Keep your hands folded in front of you."

Snap!

"Sit perfectly still."

Snap!

"Fabulous!"

Ms. Joni went on like that for a million hundred minutes. Finally, she put the camera down.

"*You* were fabulous!" said Ms. Joni, who

probably says that to everybody. "You can go back to class. We will shoot your personal pictures after all the class photos are done."

We lined up in single file to go back to our classroom. I was just about to walk out the door when the weirdest thing in the history of the world happened. Ms. Joni came running over to me.

"Excuse me," she said. "What is your name, young man?"

"Who? Me?" I asked. "My name is A.J."

"Not anymore," said Ms. Joni. "From now on, your name is . . . Fabulo."

WHAT?!

Ms. Joni was looking at me really weirdly.

"You're *perfect*!" she said, walking around me. "You have the look!"

"Huh?" I asked. "What look?"

Ms. Joni picked up her camera and started snapping pictures of me.

"I've been waiting my whole life to find a young man who looks like you," she said. "And here you are. You are Fabulo! I'm going to make you a star!"

Andrea had on her mean face.

"Star?" I asked. "W-what are you going to do to me?"

"She's gonna make you into a male model, dude," Ryan told me.

"Oh no, not just a model," said Ms. Joni. "Fabulo will be the first male *super*-model!"

"But I don't *want* to be a supermodel!" I told Ms. Joni.

"You were *born* to be Fabulo," she replied as she took more pictures of me. "There's no point in fighting it. Just look at those cheekbones! They're perfect!"

I covered my cheeks with my hands.

"B-but . . . but . . . but . . ."

Everybody was giggling because I said "but," which sounds just like "butt" even though it's missing a "t."

"Dude, being the first male supermodel will probably pay *big* bucks," Michael told me. "And all you have to do is pose for some dumb pictures. This could pay for your college education."

"But I don't *want* to get a college education!" I protested.

"You could build a skate park with the money," Ryan told me, "or a video game arcade. You'll be able to buy whatever you want, man!"

"How much money are we talking about?" I asked.

"Hundreds!" said Michael.

"Thousands!" said Ryan.

"Millions!" said Ms. Joni.

"Bazillions!" said Neil.

I don't even know if bazillions is a real number. We never learned about bazillions in math.

Andrea was standing there the whole time with her arms crossed.

"That's not fair!" she said. "Arlo doesn't even *want* to be a model."

But Ms. Joni wasn't paying any attention to Andrea. She couldn't stop staring at me and taking pictures.

"What do you say?" she asked me. "Do you want to be Fabulo, the first male supermodel, or do you just want to be some plain old boring kid?"

I didn't know what to say. I didn't know what to do. I had to think fast. This was the hardest decision of my life. I could go on being a normal kid, or I could become the first male supermodel in the history of the world. I was concentrating so hard that my brain hurt.

Finally, I decided. I could make bazillions, and I could make Andrea jealous. All I had to do was let Ms. Joni take some dumb pictures of me.

"I'll do it!" I said. "I am Fabulo!"

The Vomitorium

It was lunchtime, so we had to go to the vomitorium.

"Welcome to Café LaGrange," said our lunch lady, Ms. LaGrange. "What can I get you for lunch today?"

"I'll have spaghetti with lots of tomato sauce," said Ryan.

"I'll have macaroni and cheese," said Michael.

"I'll have a Sloppy Joe sandwich," said Andrea.

"How about you, A.J.?" said Ms. LaGrange. "Would you like some peas today?"

"No thank you," I told her. "I don't like peas."

"Oh come on," she said. "Give peas a chance."

Then she started singing that dumb song she always sings: *All we are saying is give peas a chance.*

Ms. LaGrange is strange. One time she wrote a secret message in the mashed potatoes.

I looked at the other dishes Ms. LaGrange had prepared. Beef-and-bean burritos. Sloppy Joe sandwiches. Chili Surprise. Chocolate pudding. Pickle chips. Applesauce. Tater Tots.

It all looked disgusting. Luckily, my mom packed a peanut butter and jelly sandwich for me. I just bought a carton

of milk, and we found a table that was empty.

"The guy who thought of putting peanut butter and jelly together was a genius," I told everybody. "That guy should win the Nobel Prize."

"It could have been a *lady*, Arlo," said Andrea, who still had on her mean face.

Andrea was right. A lady could have invented the peanut butter and jelly sandwich. But I wasn't about to admit that Andrea was right about anything.

"I'm so excited that you're going to be the first male supermodel, A.J." said Alexia. "You'll get to walk down a runway and everything!"

"While the planes are taking off?" I asked. "That sounds dangerous."

"Not *that* kind of a runway, dumb-head!" Andrea said, rolling her eyes. "I can't believe you're going to be a super-model, and you don't even know what a runway is."

"You're just being mean to me because you're jealous that Ms. Joni picked *me* to be a supermodel instead of you," I told Andrea.

"I am not jealous!" Andrea shouted.

"Are too!"

"R2-D2!"

"C-3PO!"

We went on like that for a while. Andrea

knew I was right, but she just didn't want to admit it.

"Hey," said Neil. "How about we play football in the playground during recess?"

"Sure," said Ryan.

"Count me in," said Alexia.

"Great idea," said Michael.

"Uh, I'm not in the mood," I said.

Everybody looked at me.

"What's the matter, A.J.?" asked Alexia.

"I just don't want to play football today," I told her.

"But you *love* playing football," Ryan said. "What's the matter, dude?"

"Okay, okay," I admitted. "Ms. Joni is going to be doing a photo shoot with me this afternoon. I don't want to get my hair messed up."

Everybody started laughing, even though I didn't say anything funny.

"Are you kidding, A.J.?" asked Neil. "You're really afraid of messing up your hair?"

"How about we play on the monkey bars instead?" suggested Alexia.

"Yeah!" said Ryan and Michael. "The monkey bars are cool."

"You guys go ahead," I said. "I'll stay in here. If I fell off the monkey bars, I might damage my face. If I broke a cheek-bone, my male modeling career would be over."

"Oh come on, A.J.!" said Michael. "You're not going to break a cheekbone."

"Not today, guys," I said. "Sorry."

Now Andrea wasn't the only one who had on a mean face. *Everybody* was looking at me with mean faces.

"You've changed, man," said Ryan. "You're not the same A.J. that I used to know."

"Yeah," said Michael. "Ever since you became the first male supermodel, you're no fun anymore."

"What?!" I said. "I'm not even a supermodel yet!"

"It's only a matter of time," said Alexia. "You're all full of yourself now."

Well, of *course* I was full of myself. I was entirely made up of *me*. I *had* to be full of myself. I couldn't very well be full of somebody *else*.

"I remember the good old days when you were cool, A.J.," said Ryan. "You're not cool anymore."

What!? *Nobody* says I'm not cool. I'm the coolest kid *ever*. It wasn't fair. My best friends had suddenly turned against me. This was the worst thing to happen since TV Turnoff Week.

I felt a sudden rage building up inside. I don't know what came over me. I couldn't control myself. So I did the only thing I could do under the circumstances.

I picked up Ryan's plate of spaghetti and dumped it over his head.

For a second, everybody was in shock. Tomato sauce was dripping down Ryan's ears.

"Oh, snap!" said Ryan.

"You can't do that to my friend!" Michael shouted. Then he took his macaroni and cheese and pushed it into my face.

"There!" he said. "You don't look like a supermodel *now*."

"That wasn't very nice!" said Andrea. She threw her Sloppy Joe sandwich at Michael. But he ducked and it hit Emily instead. She started yelling and screaming and shrieking and hooting and hollering and freaking out, of course.

"Food fight!" somebody shouted.

I'm not exactly sure what happened after that. Things got out of control. The next thing anyone knew, the air was filled with flying food. Some second grader chucked a plate full of Chili Surprise at the kid across the table from him. A beef-and-bean burrito whizzed past my head. Neil got hit in the face with chocolate pudding. It was raining Tater Tots. Pickle chips were flying around.

Somebody took a pepper shaker and started hitting meatballs up in the air like they were baseballs. Kids were squirting ketchup packets at each other. You should have *been* there!*

Eventually, we ran out of food. Café LaGrange was a mess. All four of the basic food groups were stuck to the wall, and to us.

That's when an announcement came over the loudspeaker.

"Happy Picture Day, everyone! Recess has been canceled. We don't want you boys and girls to get dirty before your

---

*Don't try this at home, kids!

pictures are taken. Mr. Cooper's class, please report to the gym."

"Oh no!" shouted Andrea. "My face is a mess! And my hair is full of applesauce!"

"This is the worst Picture Day *ever*!" said Emily.

Fabulous News!

When our class arrived at the gym, it looked like we had been through a war. Food was dripping off everybody. My hair was all over the place. My shirt was untucked. My new suit was a mess.

My career as the first male supermodel was over, for sure. But it was okay. I didn't really want to be a supermodel anyway.

"What happened?" asked Ms. Joni when she saw us come into the gym.

"There was a food fight in the vomitorium," whined Andrea. "And now I'm having a bad-hair day. Where's a mirror? I need to fix my hair!"

"Why, is your hair broken?" I asked her.

"That's not funny, Arlo!" Andrea yelled.

"I have a cowlick," complained Michael.

"You licked a cow?" I asked him. "Gross!"

"It's not funny, A.J.!" Michael yelled.

"My pants are full of chocolate pudding!" said Neil.

"Who needs pants?" I told him. "The pictures are from the waist up anyway."

"This is no laughing matter, A.J.!" Neil yelled.

Nobody was in the mood for jokes. Everybody was upset. Well, not everybody. Ms. Joni gathered us all around her.

"Don't worry," she said. "My team of photo flunkies is going to make you all look fabulous."

At that moment, a bunch of ladies came out of the locker room. They were carrying towels and spray bottles and brushes and all kinds of junk with them. They started cleaning everybody up and combing their hair. While they were working on the other kids, Ms. Joni came over and put her arm around me.

"Fabulo, I have fabulous news!" she whispered in my ear. "Remember those pictures I took of you? Well, during lunch I emailed them to *Sports America* magazine, and they want to put you on the cover!"

"WOW," I said, which is "MOM" upside down. "*Sports America*? Cool! My dad reads *Sports America*."

"Yes," said Ms. Joni. "You're going to look fabulous on the cover of the *Sports*

America swimsuit issue!"

WHAT?!

The swimsuit issue? That's the issue of *Sports America* where they have a bunch of models running around in bathing suits! I know, because my dad hides it in the garage.

"B-but . . . but . . . but . . ."

"You're going to be fabulous!" said Ms. Joni, giving me a bathing suit to put on. "I can't wait to shoot pictures of you."

But first, Ms. Joni said she had to take yearbook pictures of all the other kids. Everybody was looking into mirrors and combing their hair.

"Can I go first?" asked Ryan as he put

on his sunglasses. "I want to look like a secret agent."

"Sure!" said Ms. Joni.

She had Ryan stand in front of a big green screen. Then she pushed a button on her computer, and a picture of a racing car appeared on the screen behind Ryan.

It looked just like he was standing in front of the car. It was cool.

Snap!

Ryan slinked around like a secret agent, and Ms. Joni took his picture.

Snap!

"Smile!" she told Ryan.

"Secret agents don't smile," Ryan replied. "Smiling isn't cool."

"Oh, yeah?" said Ms. Joni. "Then I'll tell you a joke to make you smile."

"It won't work," Ryan said. "Nobody can make me smile if I don't want to."

"What's brown and sticky?" asked Ms. Joni.

"What?"

"A brown stick!" said Ms. Joni.

That was totally not funny. Ryan didn't laugh.

"Okay," said Ms. Joni, "you have forced me to say the *one* word in the English language that's guaranteed to make any third grader laugh."

Everybody leaned forward. We wanted to know the one word in the English language that would make us laugh. We were all on pins and needles.

Well, not really. We were just standing there. If we were on pins and needles, it would have hurt.

"What word is it?" I asked.

"Do you *really* want me to say it?" asked

Ms. Joni. "It's naughty."

"Yes!" we all shouted.

"Okay," said Ms. Joni. "Here it is. The word is . . . 'UNDERWEAR'!"

Ryan cracked up, and Ms. Joni took the picture.

Snap!

She was right. We all cracked up when she said the word "underwear." It's the one word in the English language that's guaranteed to make any third grader laugh. Nobody knows why.

Ms. Joni let everybody pick costumes and props out of a big box and then had them stand in front of the green screen. She could project just about any background on it. Michael stood in front of the White House holding a soccer ball. Neil stood on a mountaintop with a sombrero on his head. Andrea stood in the middle of a forest holding a teddy bear. Everybody's picture looked different. It was cool.

"Fabulous!" said Ms Joni. "I think we're just about finished with your class. There's just one more student I need to shoot. . . . Fabulo!"

Photobomb

I came out of the locker room wearing the bathing suit Ms. Joni had given me, and everybody went nuts. They were all whistling and hooting and hollering.

"Do I *really* have to wear this?" I asked.

"You look fabulous, Fabulo!" said Ms. Joni.

"And remember," said Ryan, "you're going to make bazillions."

A bunch of Ms. Joni's flunkies swarmed all over me. They put some stinky gunk on my hair, and then they combed and blow-dried it. It looked weird. Ms. Joni gave me a surfboard and told me to stand in front of the green screen.

She pushed a button, and a picture of the ocean appeared on the screen so it looked like I was standing on the beach. Next, she turned on bright lights and a big fan, and pointed them at me. I was blinded, and my hair was blowing all over the place.

"This will make it look like you're on

a windswept tropical paradise," Ms. Joni said as she picked up her camera. "They love that at *Sports America*. Okay, let's make some magic, people!"

"What should I do?" I asked.

"Just be your fabulous self, Fabulo," she replied.

I moved a garbage can to the front of

the screen and put the surfboard on top of it. Then I climbed up and pretended to be surfing. Ms. Joni took the picture.

Snap!

"Fabulous!" shouted Ms. Joni. "Now drop your chin, Fabulo."

"I can't drop my chin," I told her. "It's attached to my head. How am I supposed to drop it?"

"Leg up," shouted Ms. Joni.

I put my leg up.

Snap!

"Not there. *There.*"

Snap!

"That's fabulous! Tilt your head to the right."

Snap!

"No, a little left."

Snap!

"Smile."

Snap!

"Now frown."

Snap!

"Put the surfboard on your head."

Snap!

"Look like you just tasted ice cream for the first time."

Snap!

"Now look like you just ate some food that's past its expiration date."

Snap!

"Look like you just found out there's no school tomorrow."

Snap!

85

"Look like your dog just died."

Snap!

"Fabulous! The camera loves you! You're an *animal*, Fabulo! Pretend to be a tiger."

"I thought you just wanted me to be myself," I said.

"Be yourself," said Ms. Joni, "but with more teeth."

Snap!

"A little *more* teeth."

"These are all the

teeth I have!" I yelled.

Snap!

It went on like that for a million hundred minutes. I was exhausted. But it would be worth it to be a famous supermodel making bazillions.

That's when the strangest thing in the history of the world happened. Ms. Joni put down the camera. It looked like something was wrong.

"What's *that*?" she said, pointing behind me.

I turned around.

Out of the corner of my eye, I spotted something. Or somebody. There was movement.

It was big.

It was hairy.

It was scary.

And it was running away.

It could have been Bigfoot. It could have been an alien from another planet. It could have been *anything*.

Everybody started shouting and pointing.

"It's a monster!" shouted Ryan.

"It's a zombie!" shouted Neil.

"It's the Picture Day Zombie!" I shouted.

Chase Scenes
Are Cool

"Run for your lives!" shouted Neil the nude kid.

Okay, I *know* I told you there weren't going to be any zombies in this book. But what am I supposed to do? Zombies don't tell you when they're coming. The Picture Day Zombie just showed up! I have no control over what zombies do in their spare time.

"Grab that zombie!" I shouted.

It was too late. The zombie had already dashed out of the gym.

"Get him!" Ryan shouted.

My whole class ran out of the gym and down the hall just in time to see the zombie turn the corner.

"That zombie is *fast*!" shouted Alexia.

We chased the zombie past the science room.

Past the all-purpose room.

Past the front office.

Mr. Klutz was standing there.

"No running in the halls, kids!" he

shouted at us.

"We're chasing a zombie!" I shouted to him.

"Oh, then running is okay," shouted Mr. Klutz.

We were gaining on the zombie, but then it ran out the back door of the school into the playground.

"Grab it before it escapes into the woods!" shouted Michael.

Isn't this exciting? Chase scenes are always exciting. They should have a TV channel that shows nothing but chase scenes. I would watch that all day.

Anyway, we chased the zombie past the monkey bars and the soccer field. Finally, we caught up with it at the edge of the playground.

We tackled it and pinned it to the ground.

The zombie tried to get free, but we wouldn't let go.

It had a hideous face. I thought I was gonna throw up. But then I realized that the zombie's hideous face was actually some kind of hideous rubber mask.

"It's time to reveal the true identity of the Picture Day Zombie!" I announced.

Carefully, I lifted the hideous mask off the zombie's head. And you'll never believe whose face was underneath.

I could make you wait until the next chapter to find out who the zombie was.

But that would be mean.

I could tell you that we were all on pins and needles.

But that would be mean.

I could say there was electricity in the air.

But that would be mean.

I could say we were glued to our seats.

But that would be mean. And weird. Who puts glue on seats?

So I'll just tell you. The Picture Day Zombie was . . . Andrea!*

---

*Betcha didn't see *that* coming! The Picture Day Zombie wasn't a zombie after all. So I guess you can still say there are no zombies in this book.

Bazillions

"Eeeek!" screamed Emily. "Andrea! *You're* the Picture Day Zombie? How could you do such a thing?"

Everybody was out in the playground now, even Mr. Klutz. Andrea was crying.

"I was mad because Arlo is going to be a supermodel instead of me," Andrea admitted through her tears. "I'm sorry. I'll never do it again."

"A.J., do you accept Andrea's apology?" asked Mr. Klutz.

"Yeah, I guess," I said.

"*Ooooo!*" Ryan said. "A.J. accepted Andrea's apology. They must be in *love!*"

"When are you gonna get married?" asked Michael.

If those guys weren't my best friends, I would hate them.

When we got back inside the school, Ms. Joni had left. I figured she went to *Sports America* to give them the pictures of me. It was only a matter of time until I would be a famous supermodel earning bazillions.

But that didn't happen. A week went by and I didn't hear from Ms. Joni. I was beginning to think that Ms. Joni was a phony.

But then, a couple of days later, I was in Mr. Cooper's class when an announcement came over the loudspeaker.

"A.J., please report to Mr. Klutz's office."

"Ooooo!" Ryan said. "A.J. is in trouble!"

I walked by myself to Mr. Klutz's office. I figured he was going to tell me that I would have to leave school to go become a famous supermodel. Instead of learning math and stuff, I would be spending all my time traveling around the world on photo shoots and dancing at discos with other supermodels.

But that didn't happen either. You'll never believe who was in the office with Mr. Klutz.

Ms. Joni!

"Hello, A.J.," she said.

"A.J.?" I replied. "My name is Fabulo, remember?"

"Not anymore," Ms. Joni told me. "Those

pictures I took of you were ruined by the fake zombie. So you're not going to be in the *Sports America* swimsuit issue after all. I'm sorry."

Bummer in the summer!

"But that's not why I called you down here, A.J.," said Mr. Klutz as he opened his drawer. "The school yearbook is in."

"Cool!" I said. "Can I see it?"

Mr. Klutz took out the yearbook and turned to the photo of the whole school.

"Can you explain this, A.J.?" Mr. Klutz asked me.

"Explain what?"

"I see your face on *this* side of the photo," he said, pointing to the picture, "and then

I see your face again on the *other* side of the photo."

I didn't know what to say. I didn't know what to do. I had to think fast.

"Uh . . . one of those two guys isn't me," I finally said. "That's my twin brother. His name is . . . P.J."

"P.J.?" said Mr. Klutz. "I didn't know you had a twin brother."

"Oh, yeah," I told him. "P.J. was just visiting that day. He lives in . . . Antarctica."

"Why does your twin brother live in Antarctica?" asked Ms. Joni.

"He . . . uh . . . lives with a family of penguins," I explained.

"Um-hmm," said Mr. Klutz. "So when will we get to meet this twin brother of yours?"

"He, uh, went back to Antarctica," I explained. "The penguins were hungry."

"I see," Mr. Klutz said.

I think he believed my story. He gave me the yearbook and said I could go back to class.

Out in the hallway, I flipped through the yearbook to see what my surfing picture looked like. I found the page with my name on it. And you'll never believe in a million hundred years what it said above my name.

WHAT?!

Oh, yeah. I guess I forgot to turn in my Picture Day money. The envelope was still in my backpack.

* * *

That's pretty much what happened. Maybe Ms. Joni will stop saying "fabulous" all the time. Maybe that family of zombies will get out of our vacuum cleaner. Maybe the girls will start coming to school with laundry bags over their heads. Maybe we'll have to try on bananas before we buy them. Maybe my mom will blow her nose into her purse. Maybe Ryan will stop wearing diapers. Maybe Emily will rob a bank and go skiing. Maybe supermodels will use their superheat vision to warm up their food. Maybe I'll have my cheekbones removed. Maybe I'll get to walk down a runway while the planes are taking off.

Maybe I'll figure out a way to explain why my twin brother lives in Antarctica with the penguins.

But it won't be easy!*

---

*If you liked this book, tell your friends. If you didn't like it, don't tell anybody.